In the Tall, Tall Grass

For my Father and Mother, with love

Copyright © 1991 by Denise Fleming. All rights reserved.
Published by Scholastic Inc., 730 Broadway, New York, NY 10003, by arrangement with Henry Holt and Company, Inc.

12   0 1 2/0

Printed in the U.S.A.   08

First Scholastic printing, September 1992

ISBN 0-590-46104-4

In
the Tall, Tall Grass

Denise Fleming

SCHOLASTIC INC.

New York Toronto London Auckland Sydney

In the tall, tall grass...

caterpillars lunch

hummingbirds
sip

strum, drum,

bees hum

crack,

snap,

wings flap

pull, tug, ants lug

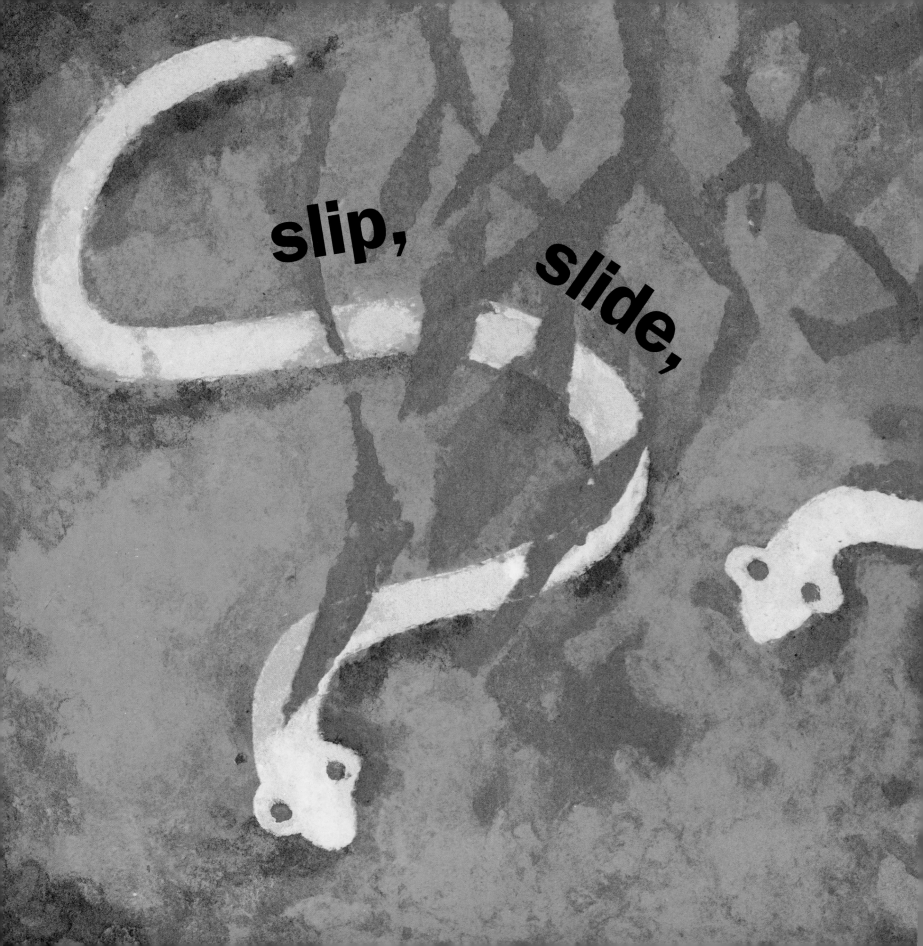

snakes glide

scratch

skitter, scurry,

beetles hurry

tongues

snap

hip,

hop,

ears

flop

stop, go,

fireflies glow

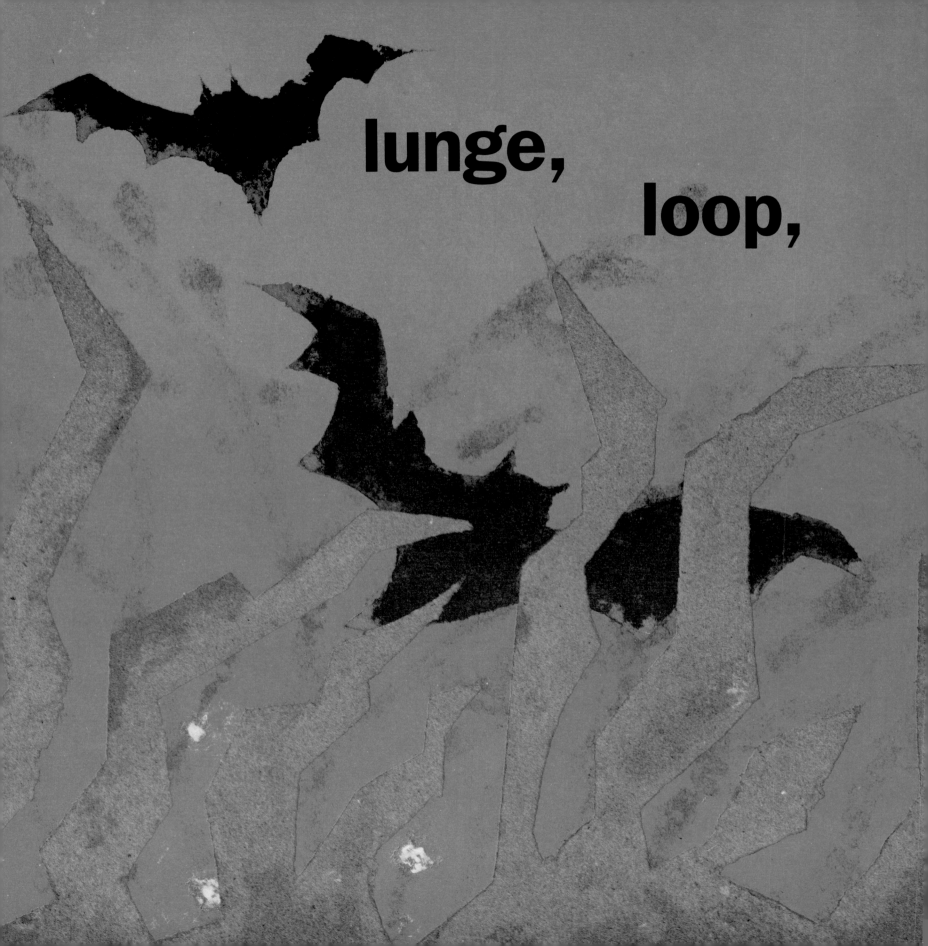

lunge,

loop,

bats

swoop.

Stars bright,

moonlight...

good night,
tall, tall grass.